AN AMERICAN FAMILY™ BOOK EIGHT: 1920

# A Test of Loyalty

## S. D. JONES

FEARON EDUCATION
a division of
David S. Lake Publishers
Belmont, California

# AN AMERICAN FAMILY™ SERIES

Book One: Colony of Fear
Book Two: A Matter of Pride
Book Three: Two Kinds of Patriots
Book Four: The Journey Home
Book Five: Fortune in Men's Eyes
Book Six: The Debt
Book Seven: A Splendid Little War
**Book Eight: A Test of Loyalty**

*Cover illustrator: Sara Boore*

An American Family is a trademark of David S. Lake
Publishers. Copyright © 1989 by David S. Lake
Publishers, 500 Harbor Boulevard, Belmont, CA
94002. All rights reserved. No part of this book may
be reproduced by any means, transmitted, or trans-
lated into a machine language without written
permission from the publisher.

ISBN 0-8224-4758-4
Library of Congress Catalog Card Number: 88-81527
Printed in the United States of America
**1. 9 8 7 6 5 4 3 2 1**

# Contents

**FAMILY TREE**

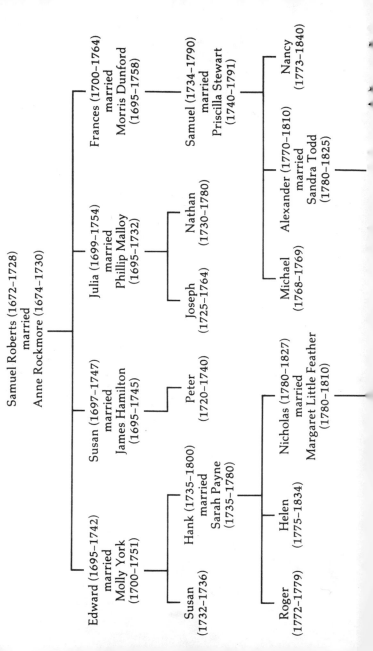

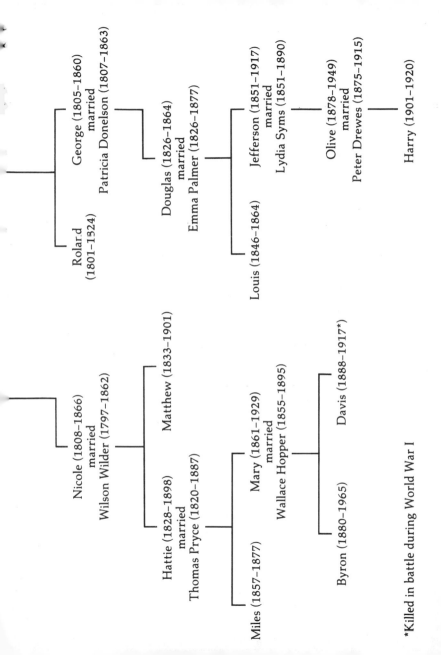

George (1805–1860)
married
Patricia Donelson (1807–1863)

Roland
(1801–1824)

Douglas (1826–1864)
married
Emma Palmer (1826–1877)

Louis (1846–1864)

Jefferson (1851–1917)
married
Lydia Syms (1851–1890)

Olive (1878–1949)
married
Peter Drewes (1875–1915)

Harry (1901–1920)

Nicole (1808–1866)
married
Wilson Wilder (1797–1862)

Matthew (1833–1901)

Hattie (1828–1898)
married
Thomas Pryce (1820–1887)

Mary (1861–1929)
married
Wallace Hopper (1855–1895)

Miles (1857–1877)

Davis (1888–1917*)

Byron (1880–1965)

*Killed in battle during World War I

# A Young Man Heads West

The train ride to Oregon was a peaceful one. Too peaceful for restless, young Harry Drewes. His mother, Olive Dunford Drewes, had seen to it that he got the best compartment. She always made sure he was well fed and looked after.

The owner of the train line was a friend of Olive's. She had written him to make sure his people would treat Harry well.

Harry watched the plains of Nebraska go by. He felt sorry for himself. This was not the trip he had hoped for. He had wanted adventure—not the porters and the room service. Back in New York, he had pictured himself riding in a freight car. How else would he be able to write about life?

Instead, the velvet on the seat and the clacking of the rail kept putting him to sleep.

Though he felt guilty, he allowed himself the rest. But he was determined to stay awake through the Rockies. This was the West! It might not be the wild and wide-open West of a half century ago. After all, this was 1920. But to Harry it was all new and very exciting.

How often had he heard of Hattie Pryce's life, growing up in the West more then 70 years ago. Harry had never known this woman, who had died long ago. But Hattie's daughter, Harry's Great-Aunt Mary, had passed along Hattie's journal.

Harry was so inspired, he started keeping his own journal. He was writing in it now. That was the purpose of this trip after all— to write about life. That was *his* purpose anyway.

As the train rolled on Harry wrote:

"All I have ever known is New York. A wilderness full of people. An island with too many bridges. I've known only cars, trolleys, noise and hustle-bustle. Riding on this train I am free. I am beginning my adventure . . ."

His mother had *other* ideas, of course. But she was not on the train. So Harry was free to do as he wished.

Many images of Oregon filled his head. He could almost see the rolling hills, bright sunshine, and open spaces. He wondered what the paper mill would look like. Would the workers there like him? Would he like them?

Would they be a rough and tumble sort of people? Would they have stories to tell? He hoped so. To 19-year-old Harry Drewes, life was a great story about to unfold. And he would be its hero.

The train rode on, with the sound of clicketyclacks and whistles filling Harry's head. It wouldn't be long now.

The train reached Redfield two days later at 4:00 P.M. Carl Franklin was already waiting for Harry when he stepped down from the train.

Harry recognized Franklin from his mother's description. "Tall, thin, like a beanpole," his mother had said. "And he has dark hair and a big, dark mustache that covers his upper lip."

At first glance, Harry thought he was a rather hard chap. But as they walked out of the train station, Carl smiled. He took Harry's luggage and warmly patted him on the back.

"Welcome Harry," said Carl. "Come with me. You must be hungry."

Harry didn't have a chance to answer, for Carl was already leading him toward a horse and buggy.

"Sorry," said Carl. "There are not many automobiles here in Redfield, Oregon. We still get around the old-fashioned way." He laughed and motioned for the driver to get going.

Harry couldn't help staring at the driver. He was an odd man, distant and cold—and big. But his eyes were small and filled with suspicion. He had an ugly scar on his right cheek. Carl noticed that Harry was staring.

"Oh, don't mind Josh here," Carl said to Harry. "He's my right-hand man. Don't talk much, but he's strong as an ox. Right, Josh?"

Carl slapped the driver hard on the back, but the big man didn't turn around. He seemed to take no notice of Harry or Carl.

Carl Franklin lived just a few blocks from the train station in a large and important-looking house. A porch wrapped around the front and there were large double doors to the entrance. Harry liked the house right away. He had lived in an apartment in the city his whole life.

Harry changed clothes and washed up as soon as he arrived. When he came down-stairs, he saw that the dinner table was set and a maid was bringing out food.

"Come on, Harry," Carl said. "Your mother wrote and told me you eat like a horse. Is that true?" He winked and smiled.

"Well, I—"

"I hope so. I have the cupboards all stocked. Don't disappoint me."

Carl motioned for Harry to sit, as he began to cut a large roast.

"So tell me," said Carl, "how's your family? How's Olive?"

"My mother's fine, thank you," said Harry.

"She tells me you want to learn some management skills."

"Actually, I—"

"Couldn't have come to a better place," said Carl. "The mill here employs 350 men full time, and many of their family members as well. I do a pretty good job of keeping them in line. But if your mother thinks I could use a little help—"

"No, no. It's not that," Harry said quickly. "Mother thinks the mill is going fine. Really. It's just that ever since Grandpa Jefferson was killed—"

For the first time Carl frowned. He looked angry. "Jefferson was a good man," he said. "It pains me to think that some drunken unionists killed him. Bomb blast, wasn't it?"

"Yes," Harry answered. "But they never really proved who—"

"It was the workers. Bet on it. Not all of them are shifty and lazy, but the ones who are, you've got to watch like a hawk. Let your grandpa's murder be a lesson to you, son."

Harry was only 19, but he never liked being called "son." "Actually, one of the reasons I came was to get to know the workers," Harry said. "I want to see how other people live, to get my hands dirty."

"Well," said Carl, "I see you are your father's boy as much as your mother's. It's the artist in you. Talk to the men as much as you like. But if you're here to help *me*, then my advice is not to get involved with them. Getting too chummy with your employees is no good. It'll only cause trouble. The workers here respect only fear. You try to act like one of them, and they'll eat you alive."

There was little use in talking, Harry felt. Carl's feelings about workers seemed to be set. Carl continued to talk on and on about the workers and unions and radicals. Harry sat in silence.

At bedtime, Harry walked upstairs to his room. Tomorrow would be a busy day at the mill. Harry wanted to be ready for it.

His bed was soft and comfortable. Very comfortable, indeed, thought Harry. He had been comfortable all his life. His whole life had been soft. Something inside him longed to break free. He was determined to get past all the velvet and silk.

Before falling asleep, Harry wrote one last entry in his journal:

"Arrived in Redfield. Mr. Franklin seems nice. Haven't seen the business or the workers yet. How odd it seems to be in the middle of this wild country and yet live in such luxury! Tomorrow, I meet the people who labor at the mill. I am nervous, but excited."

# Meeting the Workers

Harry's education in life began the next day. He found the paper mill to be a hard place. As the days and weeks went by, Harry learned more and more about the mill. He learned how it worked, and how Carl managed the people. Harry found him to be a tough man who treated his workers harshly. Still, with help from Josh, Carl kept the mill running like a clock. Harry found time to speak with only a few workers. Carl never let him get too close to them.

One morning, after breakfast, Carl showed Harry the company's books.

"I do most of the work myself," Carl said proudly.

Harry didn't take much interest in numbers, but he could guess why Carl was showing him the books. He wanted to let Harry know that he was running the business well. Carl knew that Harry often wrote home. He wanted Harry to give a good report.

After leaving Carl, Harry walked outside and looked around. He never liked the look of the mill. Of course he had seen his grandfather's factories, warehouses, and mills before. He had often toured them with his mother. But they were in the city. Buildings such as these seemed to belong to the city landscape.

The mill here was different. It too was made of dark red bricks and had gray streets. In the city, these colors all went together. But in the country, the mill looked out of place. It looked huge and angry against the rolling green hills, Harry thought.

And the smell! The smell of the paper mill was awful. Harry never could get used to it.

"This mill is a regular powerhouse," Carl said. "First trees are cut down and stripped. It's the wood pulp method. A bit old-fashioned, I know, but it's all mechanical. The wood is bleached, washed, and refined—all here."

By now the mill was a familiar sight to Harry. But he remembered the first time he had seen it. From the outside, the place had looked empty. No one walked around the grounds—they weren't allowed. At the mill, you either worked, ate, or went home.

Once inside, Harry couldn't believe his ears. The noise was hard to take. He thought back to the factories in the city. He remembered they had been noisy too. But this was different. Just outside the birds were chirping. The wind was rustling through the trees. Inside, Harry had to put his hands over his ears. A person could go deaf.

Now, weeks later Harry knew his way around the mill pretty well. He walked by the area where they cut the wood. Saws whined and snarled here. Harry kept on walking. The next area was noisy, but nothing like the last place. Carl walked up and handed him a mask.

"Here, put this around your mouth," he said, then pointed to his chest. "Saves your lungs," he explained. Harry saw the logic in that. Here, they steamed the wood before crushing and beating it. Sawdust filled the air and foul smelling steam hung everywhere.

Harry looked at the workers and they stared back, scowling through suspicious eyes. He wondered what they were thinking. Then he realized that the workers were not wearing masks.

Later Harry was watching the cooking process when Carl called to him. He wanted to see him in the office. But Harry couldn't move. He felt something stick in his throat and he started to cough. He bent forward and threw off his mask. He gagged. Josh saw him and called for Carl.

Carl and Josh took hold of Harry and helped him to an outside courtyard.

"Are you all right, Harry?" asked Carl.

Harry continued to cough and gag. Finally he was able to say that he would be fine.

Carl sat Harry down on a step. Some workers were standing outside smoking and talking on a break. When Harry looked up he saw that they were staring at him.

Carl noticed as well, and he shouted "You people have nothing better to do than gawk? Get yourselves back to work."

The workers turned away just as a man came running through the crowd. "Mr. Franklin!" he yelled. "Mr. Franklin! We've got a grindstone problem on machine six. We're going to need some help."

Carl looked upset. He looked down at Harry and said, "You feel up to taking a look with me?"

Harry wanted to go along. He didn't want to seem like a baby. But he couldn't go on. The violent coughing had left him weak.

"I think I'll just sit here for a minute," Harry said.

"All right, you take it easy," Carl said. "Just sit here till we get back. Come on, Josh.

I want you in there with me." Carl pushed Josh on ahead of him.

Harry watched as the two men went around the corner, out of sight. Once more the workers all turned toward him. Harry felt embarrassed. It was like being the new kid in class. They all looked at him but no one said a word. A few minutes passed like hours. Harry wanted to introduce himself, and if he had found one friendly face he would have.

Then a woman walked out of the group of workers. Harry figured that she was only a few years older than he was. She was fairly short, just over five feet. Her eyes were green and full of life. She wore a simple navy blue dress and a handkerchief covered her head. The most striking thing about her was her bright red hair.

"You the owner's kid?" she asked him plainly. Her boldness took Harry by surprise.

"Yes," said Harry. "How did you—"

"You've been here a while now. People find out. We're not as stupid as Franklin

thinks we are. I'm Bernadette O'Connor."
She offered her hand. Harry shook it.

"Hi. My name is Harry Drewes." The skin
on her hand felt tough and hard, like leather.
Not at all like the hands of the young women
he knew in New York.

"You're going to be all right," she told him.
"You took in a good amount of the dust. If
you're not used to it, it can hurt you bad."

Several other people seemed to gain the
confidence to come forward, too. They made
a half circle around Harry and looked down
on him.

Harry saw how tired and worn their faces
were. It was hard to tell just how old they
might be.

"I'm feeling much better," he told them.

"That's because you had a mask on," she
suggested.

"Yes," said Harry. "Why don't all of you
wear masks?"

The people standing over Harry sneered.
"Yeah, Bernadette, how come we don't?" a
few of them asked in mock wonder.

Bernadette gave Harry a kind smile. She said simply, "I think you'd better ask Mr. Franklin about that."

"Or your mother," said another voice from the crowd. Then a large man with a scruffy beard stepped from the crowd. His face was hard and dark. A front tooth was missing and his right eye was swollen.

"Go ahead," he said. "Ask your mother why the workers don't wear masks. She'll tell you they ain't worth it, that's why. Workers are no better than animals."

Some of the others grumbled. Harry couldn't tell if they were agreeing or disagreeing with the man.

"He doesn't make the rules, Nick," said Bernadette.

"No," the man snarled. "But he has a rich life because of them. That much is true."

Once more the people grumbled. This time, Harry knew they were in agreement.

"What I wouldn't give for half of what this kid had for breakfast this morning," someone said. The others laughed and nodded.

"I bet it could feed my whole family for a week," another moaned.

"A month!" another replied with a sneer. As the crowd grew louder and angrier, Bernadette jumped onto a bench.

She cried, "Listen to you! You're all crying like a bunch of babies. Picking on this lad isn't going to change your lot. This is what I've been preaching to you all along.

"Growling won't help. You moan and you cuss at your wives, husbands, and kids. You tell them how terrible your life is and how you hate it in this prison of a work place. That makes you feel better. You get all nice and warm and cozy inside because you've let out your anger. But you haven't gained anything, or changed anything. You just made your home life worse. The job stays the same."

"Tell them, Bernadette!" a voice shouted.

But someone else said, "Keep it down, Bernadette. You want Franklin to hear you?"

"Yes," she said angrily. "He does hear already. But someone's got to make him *listen*. If you want change, you have to demand it.

If you don't, things will go on the way they always have. So stop kicking your dogs and start fighting where it counts."

The workers cheered and clapped their hands. Then Harry heard a shrill whistle. Everyone looked over to their left. A little man in a newsboy cap was waving a red hankie. Harry knew it was some sort of signal.

The crowd of workers began to split up. They walked away just as Carl and Josh turned the corner. Nick helped Bernadette down from the bench.

Harry saw the angry look on Carl's face. He stared at the workers as they walked back into the mill and then looked over at Bernadette and Nick.

Nick bent down and whispered to Harry. "You tell Franklin and his bodyguard anything about this, boy, and you and I will have a little chat."

"Oh shut up," said Bernadette. "Let him say what he likes."

She turned to Harry and smiled once more. "You're welcome at the mill anytime," she said. "You have a right to be here, too. No one here really blames you. If they do, then they're wrong."

Harry had never met a woman with so much spirit and life. She seemed unafraid and strong. This woman was not like the young ladies he had known in the city. They were all lace and silk. All secret looks and glances. Bernadette seemed fearless.

She let out a friendly laugh and backed away. But she backed right into Josh. She turned and saw the giant man staring down at her.

"Why, hello Josh," she said. "Fancy running into you," she added smiling.

Carl turned to Harry and said, "I see you met the O'Connors. I thought I heard some cheering. Speaking in public again, are we Bernadette?"

"No," said Harry quickly. "She was just welcoming me. She made a nice speech and the others applauded."

"How nice of her. She often says things that make the others applaud and cheer," Carl told him.

Nick said, "She's got a gift—a gift for getting people excited." Then Nick looked right at Carl and said, "And when people get excited, they can do some amazing things."

Nick and Carl glared at one another. Harry did not know what was going on between them. But whatever it was, it frightened him. The two men seemed as though they were trying to kill one another with angry looks.

"Just get back to work," Carl snapped. "I don't pay you two to make speeches. I pay you to make paper. Now get going!"

Bernadette started to walk back to the mill but Nick stood firm against Carl.

Bernadette called back in warning, "Come on, Nick."

Nick stood his ground. Then Josh took a step forward. Carl said to Nick, "After last week, I'd have thought you'd be a little more willing to do as I ask."

Harry looked at Nick's face. Had he been beaten up by Josh? Whatever had happened between them, Nick did not seem bothered by it now.

At last Bernadette grabbed Nick by the arm and said, "Let's go!"

"Best listen to your sister, Nick," Carl told him. "She is indeed a smart woman."

Finally Nick backed down and headed for the mill.

Harry breathed a little easier. The stand-off had surprised him. He had no idea there was such trouble here. If only he could walk freely between Carl and the workers. If only he could come and go in both their worlds. He could learn so much!

# Bernadette Again

Walking back to Carl's office Harry said, "I didn't realize things were so tense here."

Carl was still angry from the scene with Nick. He snapped, "What do you mean, tense? Why that was just a little problem—nothing that me and Josh can't handle. Don't you go telling your momma that things are boiling around here."

"I didn't mean it like that," Harry said. "I know workers and managers don't always get along. It's just that—"

"Me and the workers, we get on fine," Carl said. "And that's a fact. It's just that those O'Connors are born troublemakers.

They stir everybody up. They get 'em all worked up and hot!"

Harry decided it was best to say no more. But he had to laugh to himself. Carl was a lot like Harry's grandfather, Jefferson. Once he got going, there was no stopping him. There was no sense arguing with a man like that.

"Now," said Carl, "if you're here to learn the business, I can teach you plenty. I'll show you about working payroll. Then we can go over organizing the shifts. But you won't learn anything dwelling on scenes like that one. Sorry you had to see that at all. We got a peaceful community here. We run a tight ship, too."

"I know you do," Harry replied as they reached Carl's office.

"Well then . . ." Carl walked over to the bookshelf. He took out three large leather volumes.

Harry frowned. He did not like the thought of spending the next few hours with dusty old books. Harry had made a deal with

Olive, his mother, to stay at the mill all summer. There would be plenty of time for looking at the books later.

"You know," Harry said, "I think I'd just like to have a walk first. Get some fresh air before I start."

"Suit yourself," said Carl with a shrug. "Just keep out of the way of the O'Connors. And watch yourself around the machinery. The last thing I need is for you to hurt yourself. Your mother would have my hide."

"Don't worry," said Harry. "I'll be fine. I promise."

Harry was glad to get away from Carl's fussing, and he was happy to hide from Josh's watchful eye. Josh made him nervous.

After Harry left Carl's office he saw Bernadette sitting in a hallway. She was sitting with an older woman whose hand was bleeding. Bernadette was wrapping a rag around the woman's fingers.

"Is she all right?" asked Harry.

Bernadette nodded, but said nothing.

"Can I get Mr. Franklin?"

"No," said the woman quickly. "Leave him out of this. We can manage fine without him . . . or you."

Bernadette smiled at Harry and eased the tension. "This is Sarah. I'm taking care of her just fine."

"Then at least let me get you the doctor," Harry said.

"Doctor," Sarah said. "Hah!"

"There is no doctor or nurse at the mill," Bernadette replied. "There's one in town. But that would mean taking the day off to see him. And that would mean Sarah loses a day's pay. The doctor might even tell her to stop work for a while. No one can afford to do that."

"Save your voice for the town hall tonight," said Sarah.

"No doctor?" asked Harry. He was amazed. There were nurses at all the family's mills and factories back East. Some even had doctors on call.

"We had a doctor," Bernadette said. "Then Mr. Franklin got rid of him. Cost too much, he said. The doctor made too many demands. He wanted the sick and hurt to stay away from work. Franklin didn't like that. So the doctor didn't last long."

Sarah looked cautiously around the hall. "I'd best get back inside," she said. "If the floor boss catches me I'll be out for sure."

"This is silly," said Harry. "You act as though this is some sort of prison. Surely things can't be that bad."

"You're a young man," said Bernadette. "You have a lot to learn. Why are you here anyway?"

Harry helped Bernadette to her feet and walked her down the hall. He said, "I wanted to go West. To see life and be on my own. My mother wanted me to stay home and learn the business. So this trip was a kind of middle ground. I'm here to learn the business from Carl—and whatever I can from life."

"Well," said Bernadette, "you came to a fine place to learn about life. The people here are real and good. But as for learning anything from Mr. Carl Franklin, heaven help you."

"Does everyone feel the way you do about him?"

"Everyone who dares to feel anything anymore. Everyone who hasn't given up hope."

"You seem to give them hope," said Harry.

"Yes—I do. But I want to give them more than that. So I preach to them any chance I can. I tell them they don't have to be victims of Carl Franklin.

"Not all managers are bad," Bernadette went on. "Not all mill owners are bad. There are good places to work, I figure. Why not make it good here?

"People need to stand up, to fight back," she said. "I want to see they get what's fair, that's all. And if you want to learn something of life, remember this: Treat people fairly and make sure they treat you the same way. That's what I believe."

Bernadette and Harry walked down the hall to large double doors. Harry heard the noisy rumblings of the machines. He could see the haze of the dust in the air.

"I've got to get back to work," she said.

"Will Sarah be all right?" asked Harry.

She nodded yes.

"What did she mean, 'save your voice for the town hall'?"

Bernadette looked around cautiously. "The others would tar and feather me if they knew I told you. But I think you're a good man. We're having a meeting at the town hall tonight.

"I'm going to burn their ears," she said with a twinkle in her eyes. "I'm going to stir them up something fine. And get them to see that they have rights in the work place."

Bernadette moved to open the giant double doors. She stopped and turned to Harry. She said, "I'm counting on you to keep that to yourself young man."

Harry promised he would. He watched her as she disappeared behind the door into the haze-filled room.

Harry turned from the doors and saw Josh. The big man half-smiled at Harry and walked around a corner. Harry wondered how much he had heard.

# Blood Stains in the Night

That night after dinner, Harry asked Carl for a ride into town. He wanted a chance to get out and hear Bernadette speak.

"What do you want in town?" asked Carl.

"Oh, just to look around and see the sights. I haven't yet seen the town at *night*."

"The sights of Redfield?" Carl laughed. "There are just a few saloons, a bank and a blacksmith—nothing for you to bother with. Besides, the town at night is no place for a decent young man. After sunset the workers from the mill turn it into a wild west town. All they do is drink and fight. And waste their money."

Harry felt like a prisoner. Carl seemed to think he was babysitting "Olive's little boy." Harry was missing out on the very thing he came west to see—life and people!

"All I want to do is go into town for a little while," Harry pleaded. "I've been here for weeks."

"As long as you're in my care, Harry, I promised your mother I'd look after you. Besides, this isn't a good night for it."

"What do you mean?" asked Harry.

"It just isn't," Carl replied, as if he expected the conversation to end then and there.

Harry wondered if Carl knew anything about Bernadette speaking at the town hall. He was too afraid to ask.

"Now, you'd best get yourself on upstairs and review those records I showed you," Carl went on. "If you expect to manage a place like this one someday, it's a chore you'll need to get used to."

Harry rose from his chair and grabbed the record books roughly. He shoved them under his arm and stormed out of the room.

Harry had been away from home for weeks. But he still felt he hadn't seen much. The workers he'd met at the mill seemed to be honest people—hard working and hard living. But he never managed to see them outside of work. What were their dreams and their goals? What did they want out of life?

Harry set Carl's log books aside. He was not about to read another ledger tonight.

Harry waited an hour until Carl came upstairs. It was nearly 10:30 P.M. Carl came to knock on Harry's door. As usual, he asked if Harry was all right. Harry said he was fine and was going to bed.

When he heard Carl close his bedroom door, Harry threw on a jacket, picked up his shoes, and tiptoed down the back stairway. The old house seemed to creak with every step he took.

Finally Harry reached the bottom of the stairs and crept out the back door. He sat on the back porch steps and put on his shoes. The night was as dark as tar. No moon shone. He carefully made his way to the barn.

When Hary reached the barn, he opened the doors and saw that the buggy was gone. The barn was empty.

Suddenly he heard the loud crack of a whip. Horses whinnied and wood rattled against metal. Then two black horses appeared like ghosts. When they galloped into the light of the house, Harry saw the buggy. Josh was driving the horses right toward him. Harry stepped aside and watched the buggy slow down, then come to rest within a few feet of the barn.

Harry saw Carl's light go on. He took hold of the horses' reins to calm them.

"What you doin' out here, boy?" snarled Josh.

"I could ask you the same thing," Harry replied fearlessly. He saw that Josh was clutching his side as he climbed down from the buggy.

Just then Carl came rushing out of the house. He spied Josh and then Harry. He looked more surprised to see Harry.

"What the devil is going on?" he shouted.

"I was just out for a stroll when I heard the noise," Harry said.

Josh stumbled toward the house and he glanced over at Harry. He looked guilty. Harry couldn't understand what was going on.

"Well don't just stand there boy," Carl shouted at Harry. "Make yourself useful. Put the buggy away."

Carl helped Josh into the house. Harry was confused. Why was Josh out so late? Harry felt lucky that he had not been caught taking the buggy. He climbed aboard and sat on the leather seat. Something shiny was reflected in the light coming from the kitchen. Harry touched it, and saw it was a puddle.

"Blood," he whispered to himself.

He looked into the kitchen. Inside, he saw Carl standing over Josh and shouting at him. Harry strained to hear, but he couldn't make out a word.

Harry checked the reins and found them wet with more blood. The whole cab, in fact, was splattered with blood.

Suddenly the night seemed darker than Harry could stand. Now he wanted nothing more than to get the buggy safely in the barn and get back indoors.

Once inside the house, Harry saw that his hands and clothes were stained with blood. What's more, the kitchen chair was also bloodied. Harry had seen Josh sitting there just minutes ago. The maid, dressed in a robe and house slippers, scurried into the kitchen.

"Is Josh all right?" Harry asked her.

"He'll be fine," she said. "Just clean yourself off outside and I'll take care of the mess in here."

"What happened to him?" asked Harry.

The maid shook her head and shooed him away. "If you know what's good for you, you'll just get yourself upstairs to bed. And don't ask any more questions."

Harry walked outside to the water pump. The night was quiet now. The horses were silent. Carl had stopped his shouting. The maid was no longer complaining about the mess.

In the distance an owl hooted sadly. The lonesome sound sent shivers up Harry's spine. He washed the blood off his hands. And he tried to get the blood out of his pants and shirt. But somehow it wouldn't wash away.

# An Angry Mob

When he woke up the next morning, Harry hoped the whole episode had been a terrible dream. Outside, the sky was blue, the weather was warm, and birds chirped in the trees. Maybe it had just been a nightmare after all.

But then Harry looked over at his clothes. He saw they were still stained a deep red.

Then Harry heard the angry voices chanting. At first the sound was like a murmur, but it soon grew louder.

Harry bolted from his bed. He ran to the window and looked down the road. He saw a group of people marching toward the house. Harry thought there must be around fifty of them—all men. As they marched closer, Harry could see that they carried clubs, bats, and pipes.

Suddenly the bedroom door flew open, banging against the wall, and chipping away some of the paint. Carl stood on the threshold.

"Stay in your room, lad," Carl said. "Just stay where you are. Everything will be all right."

Carl carried a shotgun. He checked its chambers and then stormed downstairs.

What was happening? Harry wished he knew. He was sure of just one thing— whatever happened to Josh last night had something to do with the problem this morning.

Harry threw on some clothes and sat at the window. He could see that Nick was the man leading the pack. He also saw that Bernadette's brother was crazed with anger.

The group of men shouted and raised their clubs in the air. They smashed down Carl's white picket gate and marched onto his neatly groomed lawn. Nick raised his arms high into the air and signaled the men to stop. Suddenly the crowd grew quiet.

Nick shouted, "Franklin! You and your thug Josh McKinley get out here!" Then he added, "Now!"

The other men grew bolder. They shouted and cheered all the more.

Carl Franklin walked calmly out of the house, carrying his shotgun. He stood silently before the angry crowd and listened to them jeer, whoop, and holler. Then he raised his rifle into the air and shot off a deafening blast.

The sound echoed all the way down the valley. Some of the men stopped their shouting and some backed off a step. But Nick stood his ground.

Carl looked Nick right in the eyes. "You'd best have a mighty good reason to destroy a man's property and put the fear of God into his houseguest," he said. "I don't take kindly to drunken toughs."

"One rifle won't stop all of us, Franklin," said Nick. Harry could see the hate in Nick's eyes. He looked like a man who was ready to fight—to the death.

"Well, it'll stop *one* of you," Carl said. "Who wants to be the one?"

No one spoke.

"I didn't think so," said Carl. "Now why don't you all calm down. Tell me why a bunch of healthy men choose to stay away from the mill. You all find other work?"

Nick snapped, "You'll find the answer to that question at the bottom of Clary Hill. That's where we found my sister this morning."

His sister, thought Harry. He means Bernadette. But what does he mean, "where we *found*" her?

Harry watched as Carl slowly lowered his rifle. "What happened?" he asked.

"We have our suspicions. We found Bernadette's body at the bottom of the hill. She was crushed to death when her buggy and her mule went over."

"I'm sorry to hear that," said Carl. But as soon as he spoke, the men began to grumble again. It was obvious to Harry that they didn't believe him. Harry wondered whether they should.

"I don't like to see any of my people hurt," Carl went on.

"What do you mean?" snarled Nick. "You hated her. You knew she could stir the workers up with her talk. You cut her wages, and made her work longer hours. But that didn't stop her."

"All right," said Carl, "listen to me. I'm just trying to run this mill as best I know how. I'm not the one caused your sister's death. Sounds like an act of God to me."

"Act of God?" several men shouted. They moved even closer to Carl. They were ready to strike. Carl raised his gun once more.

"Now if you get back to work, I might be willing to forget all about this," Carl said.

Then Harry saw Nick throw down his club and slowly walk up the porch stairs. He stood head to head with Carl. Carl put his finger on the trigger, ready for any sudden move.

"I ain't here to argue with you, Franklin," Nick growled. "I'm here to tell you. There were two sets of tracks on the hill where Bernadette's buggy went over. Someone else was there, all right.

"Now I'm sure you were safe and sound in that big bed of yours," Nick continued. "But your handyman, Josh, was seen at the town hall last night. He was there when Bernadette spoke to us. And he left about the same time she did. All we want is Josh."

The other men shouted their agreement.

"He's not here," Carl shouted back. "I don't keep track of Josh anymore than I keep track of you. You find him, you can talk to him."

Someone shouted, "Take him, Nick. Take Franklin till we can find Josh." Some of the others agreed.

"I say we rip the house apart," another man said. "He's hiding in there somewhere!" Several men roared their approval.

Nick turned on them and spoke. "No!" he shouted back. "That's just what Franklin wants us to do. If we go into his house, he'll get the police on us."

Then Harry watched as Nick turned back to Carl and spoke in a slow, clear voice. "I was hoping we could talk this through," he said. "I know why my sister was killed. And I think you know who did it. Well, I aim to hit you where it hurts." He addressed the men behind him.

"Men," he called, "you heard Bernadette last night. You heard what she had to say. She told us we could have a better life. She told us we should band together and demand what's fair. She called on us to strike. And I say we do just that."

The men cheered and clapped their hands. They hooted and hollered, but Carl stood firm. He fired another shot into the air.

"You'll starve before you see an extra cent," he shouted. "I have men who'll work in your place."

"I don't think so," Nick replied. "Every man, woman, and child is with us. You won't see a soul there tomorrow. That's a lot of jobs to fill."

Nick led the men off Carl's property. They trampled his fence and bushes before they marched back down the street, chanting and whooping.

Harry saw Carl running after them. He waved his fist into the air and shouted, "There are ways to solve your problems! I don't take to blackmail. You're a fool Nick O'Connor! I'll see you behind bars!"

Carl cussed and kicked the fence. He flung his rifle toward the house. "I'll not be threatened!" he yelled. "Not by any man!"

Harry ran downstairs. He called to Carl. "Are you all right?" he asked.

"The fools," is all he could say in reply. "I'll crush them. Don't they know that?"

Carl stormed past Harry and went back inside the house. Harry tried his best to pick up bits and pieces of the fence. He put them in a pile. He placed the wooden gate by the porch stairs.

He didn't know what else to do. He didn't want to go back inside, so he walked to the barn to inspect the buggy. He was surprised to see that it was gone.

"Josh!" Harry said to himself. "He's gone." He figured Josh must have taken the buggy and left during the night.

Harry walked back to his room and wrote in his journal:

"I've always said I wanted to see life. Now I don't know what I really meant by that. I've hated the way Carl has pampered and sheltered me here—just like mother had at home. Now, suddenly, the world has come crashing in on me. Is this what "life" is? It is angrier and uglier than I would have ever thought possible.

"I've said that all I wanted was just to observe life. To watch. But how long can I sit back and just look on like it is some kind of play?"

As if in answer to this question, Carl burst into his room. He seemed a bit calmer now, and more serious.

"What are you writing?" Carl asked.

"My journal," said Harry, closing his book quickly.

"You wouldn't be writing to your mother, would you?"

"No."

"Good. I'll tell her everything that happened in good time. There's no sense in upsetting her now. Besides, this fuss will blow over soon."

"Will it?" Harry asked with doubt in his voice. "We'll have to tell her sometime soon. I know Mother and I know that—"

"You just do as I say for now. I want you to go into town."

"The buggy's gone," Harry replied.

"Never mind that," said Carl. "You're a strong young man. The walk will do you good. It'll take you no more than an hour to get there."

Carl sat beside Harry. "This is your chance to prove yourself Harry," Carl said. "I need your help."

"What can I do?" Harry asked.

"I want you to go into town. Put on a hat and cloak. No one will notice you. I want you to get within a half mile of the mill. I want you to tell me what's going on there."

Harry started to protest. "Surely the police will—"

"The police have other plans for now. This is not a big town. There are not many police. Some of them will be nearby. But I need you to report to me, to tell me what the workers are planning."

"But if they see me—"

"They won't. And even if they do, they'll never harm you."

"But—"

Carl stood and walked to the door. He wasn't listening. He was about to leave when Harry stopped him.

"Carl," Harry said. "What happened last night?" Carl did not reply. Harry said, "When I put the buggy away, I found blood all over the seat and more in the kitchen where Josh sat. What happened last night? I want to know."

"That's none of your worry," Carl snapped.

"It certainly is!" Harry answered sharply as he stood and moved to Carl. "I met Bernadette. I talked with her. She was a good woman. Last night she died. And last night Josh came back hurt and bleeding. What did he do? And where is he now?"

Harry stood firm, but so did the older man. Carl said, "Harry! As long as you are under this roof, you'll do as I say. And I say, go into town."

"I don't want to take sides in this," Harry said. "This is not my—"

Carl let out a snarling laugh. "Take sides? My boy, you chose your side the day you put on those fancy clothes of yours. You chose sides the day you sat at my table and ate my food. The day you were born a Drewes, you took sides. It's a matter of loyalty. Report back to me tonight!"

Carl walked out and slammed the door shut. Harry knew that he could no longer just sit and watch life go by. Carl was right— he had chosen. It was a matter of loyalty. And that loyalty was being put to a test.

# CHAPTER 6

# The Strikers Hold On

Harry went into town and saw the strikers. As he had feared, Nick meant everything he had told Carl. Harry was sure there would be trouble now. There was no way to avoid it.

He wished he could smooth things over. A part of him felt that he could do it, too. If only he could talk to Nick, and if he could just reason with Carl! But it was too late for that. The strike was on.

Back at Carl's house that night, Harry wrote in his journal:

"Nick and his men have set up camp near the mill. They are being joined by hundreds of other mill workers.

"Some of them are afraid that strike breakers and police will come to attack them during the night. Others worry that they will be thrown out of their homes.

"After all, it is the mill that feeds and clothes them. The mill puts roofs over their heads. If they stay away from work too long, Mr. Franklin could have their homes boarded up. But I can't believe he would do such a thing."

Within a few days, Nick and his followers got ready for anything. They set up more tents and brought in beds and stoves. Now, even if Carl did take their homes away, they would be prepared.

For two weeks they held on. For two weeks they stood as one community. Police rode by daily and threatened them. But Nick and his men stood firm.

Carl had found a few people to take up the work. But not enough. Soon the mill had to shut down.

Harry watched Carl and wondered how long he would put up with it. Every day he grew more and more quiet. He hardly talked at all anymore, even to yell and scold.

Harry tried to feel sorry for him, but he could not. He believed Carl had basically been a good man—once. But he seemed to have lost his reason and any sense of fairness. In the last week, he'd had the workers' houses boarded up.

Then, there was still the question of Bernadette's death. Every night Harry lay awake and wondered what really happened to Bernadette on Clary Hill.

Had she died in an accident? Had Josh killed her and somehow hurt himself as well? Harry realized he might never know for certain. But as each day passed, he grew more uncomfortable with Carl. After a while Harry began to suspect Carl of causing the whole mess. Maybe Carl did not tell Josh to hurt Bernadette—but he had helped Josh to escape. He was hiding something.

"Harry!" Carl called one morning.

Harry came downstairs. He looked at Carl coldly. "What do you want?" he asked.

To Harry's surprise, Carl was in a better mood today. He seemed brighter and happier. "This is no place for a young man like you," he said. "I have a ticket for you on the first train leaving Redfield tomorrow for New York."

"That's fine with me," said Harry. "I haven't been any help to you anyway."

Carl stood and looked Harry in the eyes. "You don't like me much, do you, boy?"

"Not really," said Harry. "It seems to me the workers don't ask for much. They ask to be looked after when they get hurt. They ask for better conditions in the mill. They ask for shorter days—"

"And you don't think those demands amount to much, eh?"

Harry shook his head.

"Well, the way I see it, all that will be over tomorrow night," Carl said.

Harry's eyes narrowed with suspicion. "What happens tomorrow night?" he asked.

Carl sat back down in his rocker. He took out a big cigar and lit it.

"How long do you think it would be before the strikers started hurting *you*," Carl began, changing the subject.

"Me?"

"I don't mean physically. I mean in the pocketbook. A month? Two months? Then your momma would have to close this mill. Maybe shut down another factory. Soon, you'd be wearing rags instead of those fancy duds you wear now.

"How much," he continued, "would you be willing to give those workers from your own pocket? If it was *your* money—how many nurses would you hire? How many improvements would you make?"

"I'd do whatever I needed to. At least I hope I would," replied Harry.

"Suppose for every extra penny that you gave them, you also had to give something else up? What then?"

"What do you mean?"

"You give them a penny *and* you have to give up all your nice clothes—"

"That's silly," Harry said.

"Another penny for them means no more fancy New York apartment for you. Another penny and no more nice books. You think you'd still care then? You think you'd still worry yourself to sleep at night?"

"What's your point?" asked Harry.

"My point is that *I'm* the one who's putting my life on the line. I'm only trying to keep your momma's business from going under. And if that means waiting out those lazy ruffians, I'll do it. And if that means hiring men to . . ." Carl stopped short.

"To what?" asked Harry.

"The workers are breaking the law, son."

"What happens tomorrow night?" Harry asked. "What are you going to do?"

"I need to keep that mill open. It's my job. It's what I've been hired to do! Now you'd best pack your things."

"Get me out of the way before the trouble begins, right?" Harry said. "What are you going to do? Bring back Josh? Bring back ten more Joshes? Do to the others what he did to Bernadette?"

"That's enough," shouted Carl. "I'll bring in as many men as I need. And there will be plenty of them—you can count on that."

"Armed?" asked Harry.

Carl did not reply. He just sat there staring out the window, smoking his cigar.

Harry said, "If you think you're doing this to please my mother, you're wrong. She would never agree to bring in toughs and thugs. I'll tell her about this. Either way, Mr. Franklin, . . . you're through."

Carl blew a stream of smoke toward the ceiling. He smiled. "I don't think so. Your mother told me to do whatever I needed to do."

He handed Harry a telegram. Harry read it. It said that Carl should handle the strike in whatever way he thought best.

Harry threw down the telegram. "She doesn't know you're planning *this*. If you bring in armed men, there'll be a massacre."

"Your momma said, 'whatever.'"

"Anyway, I've written her about all this," Harry said coolly. "Once she knows the facts, I'm certain she'll see things differently."

Carl stood. The conversation was over. "The mail here is not like it is in New York," he said, smiling. "It tends to be slower in Oregon. Sometimes, it even gets lost."

Harry couldn't believe his ears. Had Carl actually taken his letters and not sent them home?

"I haven't heard from Mother since the strike began," Harry said, almost to himself. "You took my letters! You destroyed them! My mother—"

"Your mother doesn't have to live with these people, or keep them in line. This is *my* mill. These are my people. They work by my rules. I've made a name for myself in this town. I'll be mayor in another year. I'll own this town."

"So, that's what all this means to you—power. You don't care about the workers or my family, do you? This is your little kingdom and you're the mighty ruler."

"Train leaves at 7:00 A.M.," Carl replied. "It's for your own good, boy."

# The Attack

At midnight, Harry sneaked down the backstairs. He took only his and Hattie's journals with him. All his clothes and his books he left behind.

Before turning the lights out, he had written:

"Mr. Franklin said I had chosen sides the minute I was born. I do not agree. We have choices all our lives. No one is born into one single way of life. And no one is born into one single way of thinking. I don't have to be on the side of either the poor or the rich. I don't have to be on the side of the mill worker or the mill owner. I am on the side of truth and fairness. I will join whoever is right against whatever is wrong. I will join whoever is just against whoever seeks to crush justice. That is my choice. Tonight, I have made my choice."

In the darkness, Harry began his trip toward town. A little more than an hour later, he saw the mill. The sight of it at night was overpowering. It loomed out of the darkness like a sleeping giant. It looked huge and mighty.

He saw the tents on some land near the mill. The camp looked like a small city. Here and there fires were burning. People stood near the fires warming themselves. Harry could barely make out the faces of the mothers, children, old men, and young boys. But he heard many of them singing—*singing* of all things! And someone was playing a fiddle.

Most of the people just sat and waited. Some men watched. Harry figured they were waiting for trouble. He only hoped they were ready for it.

Harry walked closer and closer to the strikers.

"Halt!" someone cried. "Who is it?"

"Harry Drewes. I've come to give a message to Nick."

"That's the owner's kid," someone called out.

"Go back to your mommy—boy!" another cried out.

"I have an important message," Harry said. "Please!"

"We don't deal with messenger boys. If Franklin wants to talk let him come here himself."

Then Harry heard a familiar voice. It was Nick. "Let him come on," he growled.

The guard let Harry through.

"What do you want to tell me?" said Nick. "It must be something big. You're risking your life coming here. A few days ago I might have taken you hostage."

Harry said, "Can I talk to you in private?"

"We don't have secrets here," said Nick. "You tell me and you tell us all."

Harry looked around at the people walking toward him. He could feel their fear and their anger as they formed a circle around him. It made him very nervous.

"Mr. Franklin . . . he plans to call out men to storm your community."

The crowd stirred.

"How many men?" asked Nick.

"I'm not sure," Harry answered. "He said as many as he needed. He plans to attack the tents tomorrow night. They'll have guns I'm sure. And they mean to crush you all."

The crowd began chattering. Some women began to cry and some men cursed. Some ran to warn the others and some ran to get their weapons. But Nick stood firm.

"You believe the kid?" someone asked Nick.

Nick looked Harry right in the eyes. He stared at him for a moment, and then he said, "Yes, I do. Bernadette was a good judge of people. She took a liking to this fellow. It's Carl Franklin I don't believe. When did Franklin tell you this?" Nick asked.

"Just this evening," said Harry. "I sneaked out as soon as I could."

"And he made a point of telling you that they would attack *tomorrow* night?"

"Yes," Harry answered.

"Does he usually tell you things? Secrets like this?"

Harry thought about that for a moment. Carl had said almost nothing to him for two weeks. He had hardly said a word to Harry until tonight.

"No," Harry said. "He doesn't usually tell me much."

"Then it makes sense. We're in more trouble than even *you* thought, Harry. Though you may have saved many a life."

Nick turned to the others and said, "Franklin and his men are going to fight for the mill—tonight!"

"What?" Harry said. "Are you sure, Nick?"

Nick grabbed Harry by the shoulders and said, "Franklin was counting on you coming here to tell us this. He figured we'd sit around all night and plan for the *next* day. But we'll be ready for him!"

Nick jumped upon a wooden table and shouted at the crowd of people.

"Listen to me, all of you! All we've asked Franklin to give us is fair and honest treatment. You know that. Bernadette knew it, too. But Carl Franklin is not an honest man. Tonight he plans to take this little town by force. He plans to let us know who is in power and who isn't. Well, we'll be ready!"

The crowd let out a roar. As they were shouting, Nick stepped down and gathered a few of his men around him.

Softly he said, "This is going to be an all out battle. I know it. Get all the women and children over into the woods. Then I want every man with a hunting rifle to get it and come back here. Anyone who wants out had better leave now." No one moved.

"Then we're all in this together," said Nick.

The men began to move quickly. Within an hour, all the women and children were safely away from the camp. The men had taken every bit of furniture from the tents. They grabbed every piece of equipment they owned. They piled them up and used them as barriers.

Harry pitched in where he could. He had never fired a gun before. He didn't want to, either. But he helped the women and children get away. And he helped the men strengthen their barricades.

As he gave orders, Nick helped like everyone else. He carried weapons and drove buggies. In a few hours, Nick and the others had made the tent city as strong as it could be.

Then there was nothing to do but wait. Each man, stared into the darkness, waiting. They heard sounds every second—sounds like car engines and horses' hooves and voices. But they were just noises. Nothing happened.

The night wore on. Nick began to wonder if, in fact, Harry had been told the truth. In another hour or so it would be dawn. Some of the men had even fallen asleep.

Then the roar of an engine awoke them. It was an awful sound of metal grinding against metal. It hissed and spit like a giant steam engine. It roared like an old boiler.

"What the devil is that?" someone whispered.

The noise grew louder. Then they heard the horses' hooves. There was no mistaking the sound this time. It was the dull thunder of hooves.

"Must be a hundred of them, maybe more, Nick said.

Harry's stomach churned. He felt sure he was going to die—he could feel it in his gut. He closed his eyes and uttered a prayer. Maybe things would be all right.

The growl of the engine turned into a horrible scream. The men could see headlights like fiery dragon eyes, burning through the night.

"Get ready!" shouted Nick.

Ready for what, Harry thought. What was it? It looked like some kind of tank.

They could see the horses now. There were about 50 of them clearly visible. A row of men with clubs and rifles marched ahead of them.

Even before a shot was fired, women and children began crying. Men began to sweat and shake and a few ran away.

Harry thought about running too. He didn't know what kept him from doing it. There he was, clutching a gun he had never fired before, fighting a fight that was not really his own. He was afraid. He tried to pray again but nothing came. His mind was blank.

The armed men advanced, but they didn't fire. Harry wondered what they were waiting for. Why don't they just get it over with?

Wildly, he wondered if the armed men had been sent as a show of force. Maybe they would simply threaten. Maybe this whole mess could be avoided.

Harry had almost convinced himself of that when a hail of bullets exploded from the dragon—the armored car. As the car rolled into the camp, men scattered everywhere.

"Hold your ground!" shouted Nick. "Stay where you are. They're trying to draw your fire."

It was true. The bullets had been fired over the striker's heads. But the trick had worked. Nick's men began to fire back and leave their cover. They ran in all directions to wherever they thought were safer spots.

It looked like a hurricane of confusion was whirling through the tent city. The armored car spit more bullets and the men on horseback charged. The rest of Franklin's men rushed into the camp with torches, rifles, and clubs.

The noise was horrible. Harry picked up his gun and began to fire. He couldn't see, but he just kept firing.

Franklin's men began tossing torches into the tents. Fires sprang up almost immediately, sending people running everywhere. The men on horseback leapt over the tables, chairs, and buggies, firing at random.

Whatever order Nick had imposed on his men was gone now. Everyone was shooting without purpose. All around him, Harry saw dying men screaming for help. The fires were burning out of control. It seemed as though the entire tent city was ablaze. The heat was horrible.

The armored car ripped through the city, turned and came directly toward Nick and his men. Harry jumped and pointed toward the car. He grabbed Nick by the shoulder.

"Nick," he cried. "It's coming this way!"

Before his words faded into the air, the car spit out another hail of bullets. More men scattered, but Harry and Nick stood their ground. Only six men were left beside them—the others had been killed or had run off.

Nick signaled for the men to fall back as the armored car came closer. Harry and the others did as Nick ordered. They fell back and hid behind a row of plows and tables.

But Nick did not follow them. He stood fast and fired at the car. He just kept shooting. When he ran out of bullets he reloaded and shot again.

"Get back!" cried Harry. But Nick wouldn't listen.

The armored car fired again and again. The bullets ripped the dust and grass around Nick. Harry heard the hissing and then he heard three short thuds. Nick was hurled backwards. He staggered, then tried to get to his feet.

Harry saw that Nick had been badly hit. "They'll kill him," shouted Harry as he rushed from behind a plow. As he ran toward Nick, the car rolled closer.

Harry grabbed Nick and he began to drag him toward cover. Bullets whizzed by their heads. Harry fell to his knees. He clutched Nick by the neck and shoulders. Together they crawled nearer the barricades.

But the car was too quick for them and the men inside the car were too eager. More bullets exploded all around them. Then Harry heard another thud, and another. He felt Nick go completely limp in his arms.

The car rolled onward, racing by Harry as though the men inside it had never even seen him. Nick lay still in Harry's arms. Harry realized he was dead.

Harry saw the tents ablaze and bodies scattered all over the ground. There must be a hundred people dead or wounded here, thought Harry.

At last, the gunfire stopped. Men still ran and horses still jumped and reared. But the horrible sound of gunfire had stopped.

There was no need to shoot anymore. The battle had ended almost as soon as it had started. Nick's ragtag workers were no match for the armed men of Carl Franklin.

The armored car drove off. The horses' hooves pounded and clip-clopped away. Only a few dozen armed guards still walked about. Now and then Harry could hear a woman scream or a man cry out in pain. And he could hear the children crying all around him.

Suddenly Harry felt weak and lightheaded. His chest began to hurt and his heart began to pound. He looked down and saw that he was bleeding. He thought the blood was from Nick's wounds. But then he looked again and saw the rip in his jacket. He saw the blood oozing through his shirt. "I've been hit," he said aloud.

He staggered back to the place where he had hidden his journals. He wanted to write an entry—a note to his mother. He had to write one last note explaining things, one last note to tell her he loved her. But he hadn't the strength.

The tent city seemed to whirl around him. The blazing fires roared and hissed and he began to sweat. Then he felt chills.

He picked up Hattie's journal and opened it. How often it had given him comfort, and helped him through dark times. Maybe he could read one last page. Yes, that would make him feel better.

Harry looked toward the east and saw that the sun was rising. A new day was beginning. The last thing Harry Drewes saw was the sun breaking over the hills, it's rays thrusting long slivers of light into the valley.

He did not want to give up yet. He wanted to see this nightmare through to the end. He wanted to see the workers get what they asked for. Harry knew that Carl's days of managing the mill were over. Carl had dug his own grave. No matter what happened now, his family would get rid of Franklin. Harry told himself that the workers would get a better man. He told himself that from now on conditions would be better, safer. But what a terrible price had been paid. Dozens were dead—maybe more. Entire families had been destroyed. And all out of suspicion and fear.

# Olive's Promise

When his mother found him, Harry was still clutching Hattie's journal. He was laying face down on the ground with one arm outstretched as if he were reaching for something. For what, his mother couldn't say, because there was nothing close by to reach for. Perhaps, he was grasping for one last moment of life—a life ended all too soon.

Olive Dunford Drewes had begun her journey west more than a week before. She had read in the papers about the strike. She had wondered why her son had not written. She had hoped to step in and stop any trouble before things got out of hand.

She had arrived that very morning. But her visit was too late. It was too late to save lives, but not too late, she vowed, to make things better.

Olive took the journal from her son's cold hand. It was opened to a yellowed page. The page was torn. The date of the entry was August 21, 1853. Hattie's handwriting was rough. Olive read:

"Thomas and I have been traveling for some time now. I look forward to my new life with him in South Carolina. But I do miss the West! And how I miss brother Matthew, mother, and father. As we move on I see more and more of this country. It is a huge land. Open and wide and free. It is full of beginnings and endings. Full of life and death.

"One man comes in. He plants and builds a home. Then another comes along and builds nearby. Soon towns spring up where once there were tepees. Roads cover old wooded paths. Life is destroyed to make way for new life. Sometimes I get dizzy thinking about it all. Life here seems to move faster with every passing minute.

"But I will never forget that people make the land what it is. Their actions speak for them. I hope that they will always act for the right and for the good. Then, no matter what changes come, I know they will be changes for the better."

Olive closed Hattie's journal. Then she picked up Harry's journal from the rubble. She clutched both books close to her heart.

Olive stood and said a prayer, a prayer for Harry and for Hattie. Then she said a prayer for all the people who had died.

And finally she prayed for the living—for herself and for the workers—and for all those who would come after them.

"Changes for the better," she said aloud. "Yes. I promise you that, Harry Drewes. I promise you that."